Carnival
An imprint of the Children's Division
of the Collins Publishing Group
8 Grafton Street, London W1X 3LA

Published by Carnival 1989

ISBN 0 00 194400 2

Printed and bound in Great Britain by Collins Glasgow

THE REAL GHOSTBUSTERS™

STORYBOOK

Adapted by Maureen Spurgeon
from original TV scripts.

CARNIVAL

YOU CAN'T
TAKE IT
WITH YOU

Night had fallen on New York City. The streets were deserted, quiet and, for once, spook-free. The people of the great metropolis slept peacefully in their beds, secure in the knowledge that *should* any ectoplasmic eruption occur, The Real Ghostbusters would be there to save the world.

In Ghostbusters HQ, three of our heroes were also in bed *trying* to sleep peacefully. Winston Zeddmore had his head under the pillow counting ghosts jumping over the containment unit, Ray Stantz had his eyes shut tight and was trying to conjure up pictures of super-size-with-extra-topping pizzas. Peter Venkman was groaning. Loudly. And Egon Spengler? He was sitting up, reading the newspaper – aloud – and keeping everyone else awake.

"It's incredible really," he was saying. "The sheer nerve of it. Imagine *buying* the Empire State Building."

"Yeah – incredible," groaned Peter. "Go to sleep Egon – please!"

"It says here," Egon continued, "that this Tummel character is the richest man in America. Apparently his wealth runs to billions of dollars."

"Wrap up, Egon, " came the muffled voice of Winston from under his pillow. "Please."

Suddenly, one of their PKE meters began bleeping, and they looked round at each other, puzzled. A Psycho Kinetic Energy reading signalled the presence of some strange manifestation — but the question was — what? All had looked calm when they went to bed.

"Most peculiar . . ." murmured Egon. He went to pick the PKE meter up, but the bleeping had already stopped. "Most peculiar!"

Complete and utter silence. Then suddenly, all the alarms began echoing right through the entire building!

"The containment!" yelled Ray, already sliding down the fireman's pole to the basement, where all the ghost traps were unloaded. "Sounds like a major break!"

And, yet when Egon and Ray arrived at the containment unit

everything seemed normal. Except that is for the lights on their PKE meters winking on and off, and a powerful buzzing noise that threatened to deafen them at any minute.

Then — silence again, just like before. None of them could understand it.

Meanwhile, in the roof-top laboratory of the Empire State Building, a bent, old man in a wheelchair was giving the final orders to his very own scientist. And, boy, could he afford to! For this was R. A. Tummel himself, the richest billionaire of them all!

"Ready to attempt transit, Sir!" the scientist announced, his hand poised over a Big Switch.

"Then, proceed!" wheezed Tummel. His beady eyes gleamed as dials glowed and sparks shot out from the top of a huge, silver pyramid in the middle of the room.

The four Ghostbusters screeched to a halt outside the building in the converted ambulance they called ECTO-1. They had followed

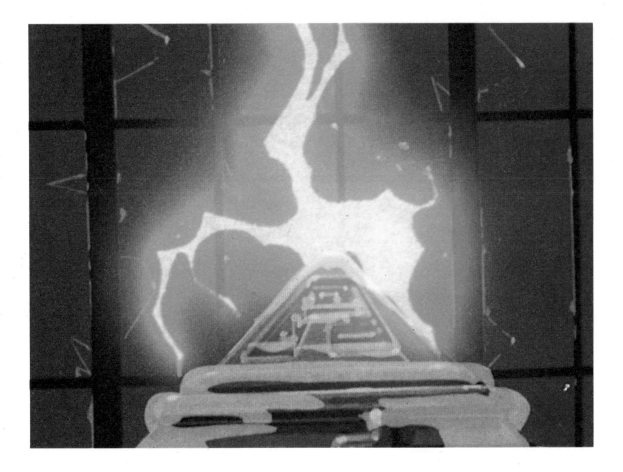

the intermittent bleepings from their PKE meters until they had arrived at the Tummel skyscraper. It seemed as though the whole town was lit by the tornado of ectoplasm shooting up into the night sky, the top of the skyscraper swathed in a strange, glowing mist.

R. A. Tummel was certainly making sure the scientist earned his keep . . .

Already, a robot-controlled fork-lift had taken a whole conveyor belt load of gold bullion, and set it beneath the pyramid. Now, high above, the scientist was at the control panel . . .

"Hurry up!" Tummel snapped impatiently. "Get on with it!"

Wave upon wave of a glowing red light surged through the laboratory, spreading all around in one mighty roar. The gold bullion began shimmering, becoming transparent . . . then surging into a golden light it shot up towards a cluster of fast-whirling clouds . . .

"We did it!" cried the scientist. "We have transmitted gold — physical matter — into the ghost world!"

"Good!" Tummel cackled in delight. "Now I'll be able to take my whole fortune with me! Send over the next load!"

"But-but, Sir . . ." stammered the scientist. "We have to check to see what effect there has been on the environment . . ."

"Environment?" screeched Tummel. "Who cares about the environment?"

"But-but, Mr Tummel . . ." Even as the man spoke, Tummel was jabbing a button on his wheel-chair. "We-we agreed that . . ."

He said no more. Two of Tummel's bodyguards had answered his call. They pounced on the scientist and dragged him away.

"Scientists!" Tummel spat out in disgust, a wrinkled hand reaching towards a portable control-box. "Who needs them?"

The roaring sound was even louder with the second lot of bullion. A steaming cloud of gold blasted up through the top of the pyramid with a noise like a thunderclap — a thunderclap merging into a chorus of unearthly wails which threatened to tear the night air apart.

The Ghostbusters had seen many, many strange things. But, never before had they seen a stream of ghostly ectoplasm shooting into the top of a skyscraper from a whirlpool of swirling cloud.

"Wh-what's that howling sound?" Peter asked at last, hardly daring to hear the answer.

"It's the wail of ghosts," Egon told him. "Hundreds and

hundreds of ghosts! Whoever opened the door to the spirit world forgot that it swings both ways!"

"Which means the ghosts are coming back out!" groaned Peter. "I don't believe it!"

Tummel could hardly believe it, either. Everywhere he looked, there were ghosts coming towards him from the direction of the pyramid, whirling and swirling around, screaming and grunting and wailing.

Lucky for Tummel, his scientist had left him well prepared. He pressed a switch on his wheelchair and a whole set of curved rods shot out from the arms, joining up above his shrivelled head like a giant, glowing phone-booth.

Another switch — and up came a Proton Gun from the back of the wheelchair, swivelling around on a tall rod, firing in all directions.

"Go on!" shrieked Tummel, enjoying the sight of so many spooks, all screaming and yelling at once, and flooding out through the door. "Beat it, you creeps!"

Down on the street, The Ghostbusters ran for their lives as a whole swarm of gruesome ghosts, ghoulies and spooks teemed onto the pavement. Egon dived into a nearby hedge for safety, Ray found himself flattened against a lamp-post.

Winston peered from behind a trash-can where he had lunged for safety.

"I think," he said, "we'd better get up there . . ."

That was easier said than done. The moment they set foot inside the building, Egon's PKE meter began buzzing like crazy — signalling the approach of four gruesome ghosts heading straight towards them!

Proton beams from four Proton Guns streaked out instantly, hitting two of the ghosts. As for the other two, they flew clean over The Ghostbusters' heads and into the darkness, mists trailing behind.

Egon took a deep breath, and looked around. "These ghosts are coming through from the spirit world by artificial means," he said. "They could break up, each fragment becoming a complete ghost . . ."

"Then, the cycle could repeat?" Peter queried slowly. "The world could become full of ghosts?"

"Yes." Egon was deadly serious. "In about fifteen hours. I think we'd better take the stairs . . ."

"Are you crazy?" demanded Peter. "It's 150 floors, and . . . Egon, why are you looking like that? Can't you do anything but point? What the . . .?"

He glanced over his shoulder and suddenly understood. A huge, giant mouth was where the lift doors had been.

"Aaaaagh!" yelled Peter, narrowly escaping a long, red tongue. All the lift doors yawned wide open to reveal huge, watering mouths, hungrily champing monster teeth, and enormous, slobbering lips.

"Come on!" Ray Stantz was bellowing. 'Get into ECTO-2!"

The ghostly cloud still whooshed up from inside the building, tossing ECTO-2, The Ghostbusters' helicopter, around like a rag doll, high above the towering Tummel skyscraper.

"We-we're fighting the magnetic pull of the ghost world!" Ray panted, struggling to keep control, and yelling above the bolts of electricity which were crackling all around, like huge forks of lightning.

Next minute – total silence. The deadly quiet made The Ghostbusters glance fearfully at each other.

"The magneto's been hit!" yelled Ray. "We're losing height!"

"Rip the wires from the instrument panel, Ray!" shouted Egon. "I'll try connecting them into my Proton Pack!"

Ray hurriedly made a jump-lead to connect up to the ignition. He turned the key, and, in the nick of time, the helicopter gave a lurch and the rotor blades began whirling again.

In a matter of moments, The Ghostbusters had landed on the rooftop. They bundled out of ECTO-2, yelling their heads off, their Proton Guns firing at the army of spooks who had been waiting for the attack.

"Okay, you guys!" roared Peter to the others, once the coast was clear. "Inside!"

The Tummel skyscraper really was some cool place. Paintings . . . statues . . . tons of stuff made of solid gold . . . But The Ghostbusters had no time for an inspection tour. They headed straight for Tummel's sky-high laboratory.

"So!" shrieked Tummel, as the alarms sounded. "I have uninvited guests!"

"Mr Tummel!" called Egon. "Could we have a word with you?"

"No!" screeched Tummel, glaring down at them from the observation balcony. "Have a word with these, instead!"

"Lasers!" gasped Winston, looking up at the ceiling, where the powerful beams were swivelling around, searching for their targets. "High power lasers! Take cover!"

They were only just in time. Winston had hardly pushed Ray away when a beam of ruby light zapped down, right where he had been standing, leaving a molten, smoking hole.

"Ha!" snarled Tummel, positively enjoying all the bangs, the explosions, the smoke and the flashes. "That should keep them busy! Time for the money to go across, I think!"

"Wow . . ." Egon couldn't help being impressed as he watched huge bundles of bank-notes glowing, becoming transparent, then being sucked up into the pyramid in a stream of gold vapour. "That's fantastic!"

"Never mind how fantastic it is!" snapped Peter. "How do we get him to stop?"

"If we could only get him to overload his equipment . . ." Egon said thoughtfully, specs gleaming. "That would block the whole works!"

Peter thought quickly, then tied a handkerchief to the barrel of his Proton Gun. "You've blown it, Tummel!" he shouted, waving the makeshift white flag. "You can send over your loot, but what about this building? Where are you going to live? They don't have

hotels over there you know. Leaving it to charity?"

"Charity?" roared Tummel. "Never! I'm taking it with me!"

The whole laboratory began throbbing with a huge roar: the deadly laser beams went berserk. Clearly, Tummel meant every word he said.

"He's overloading the equipment, Egon!" said Peter. "What now?"

But even an ace Ghostbuster like Egon Spengler could not have predicted what happened next. A stray laser shot hit the switch panel on Tummel's wheelchair, sending it straight down the ramp which led towards the pyramid!

"No! Wait!" shrieked Tummel, frightened out of his life. But, it was hopeless. With one last, loud "No-o-o-o-o . . ." the wheelchair rolled under the pyramid.

As one man, The Ghostbusters ran forward, even though, deep down, they each knew they could do nothing to help . . .

"The system's running wild!" bawled Egon.

"Shoot the controls!" bellowed Peter, taking aim along with
Winston.

"It's too late!" shouted Ray. "The system's on automatic!"

Impulsively, Egon made a grab at the ghost trap and began racing
forward, dodging the hail of laser fire. Holding his breath, he opened
the doors to the ghost trap, then pushed hard, skidding it across the
laboratory floor and under the pyramid.

Almost immediately, there was an ear-splitting warbling noise and
waves of light started to flash madly. Two laser shots almost hit Egon
before Winston managed to snatch at his belt and pull him to safety.
He was just in time. A split second later a huge chunk of Tummel's
laboratory came crashing down, and landed right where he had been
standing.

"The ghost trap should jam the transmission works!" panted
Egon, as The Ghostbusters began sprinting towards the living

quarters for safety. "I-I only hope it's enough to pull back the ghosts which Tummel released, and close the hole!"

Three deathly-white faces emerged from the living room. Only this time they weren't ghosts, they were Tummel's butler, cook and gardener, their frightened staring eyes lit by the streaks of lightning which flashed through the windows.

"Oh, thank goodness!" cried the butler. "Mr. Tummel was going to send us into the ghost world, along with all his riches!"

"Well, that's all over, now!" Egon told them, staring up at the sky, and the hordes of ghosts rising towards the distant clouds. "All the spirits are going back through the gate . . ."

"So is this building in about thirty seconds!" interrupted Peter, dragging Egon, the butler, cook and gardener towards the helicopter. For a moment, they were all thrown off balance, and Peter had to reach out to steady himself.

His hand passed straight through solid brickwork.

"This is it, Peter," Egon nodded, "The building's molecular structure is beginning to disintegrate!"

"Hurry up!" yelled Ray from the cockpit of ECTO-2. "Quick, before she goes!"

By now, the skyscraper was throbbing beneath the swirling cloud, tongues of burning vapour missing the helicopter by inches.

In near desperation, Winston ripped off his Proton Pack and flung it down towards the glowing building. The massive blast which followed lasted just long enough for ECTO-2 to break free from the deadly magnetic pull . . .

"Look!" Egon shouted. "It's Tummel!"

And, so it was, rising into the air in a cackle of mad laughter, along with all the other ghosts. Seconds later his skyscraper was sucked up, vanishing in a thunderous explosion which almost split the whole sky into two.

How Ray Stantz landed the helicopter safely, nobody ever knew.

"Now, who'd believe that?" he said dazedly. "The Tummel skyscraper, gone, and . . . Ow!" He rubbed his head indignantly. "What hit me?"

"Well, what d'you know?" grinned Peter Venkman, as bundles of notes and gold bars began showering down. "Tummel may have been a real meanie, but it seems this job's going to pay better than we ever thought!"

THE MAN
WHO NEVER
REACHED HOME

It was a strange, half-forgotten tale. How, over 100 years ago, a man named Simon Quegg strode from a roadside inn, threatening to have it closed. The innkeeper pleaded with him to change his mind. But Quegg would not listen. Instead he mounted his horse buggy, determined to leave the place at once and travel home. The innkeeper warned him of the danger of travelling on such a terrible night, when thunder rolled and lightning flashed across the sky, but it was no use.

"The devil himself can't stop me!" Quegg had ranted. "Or, may I never see home again!" And with that he hurtled off into the night.

At once a flash of lightning cracked down from the sky, hitting the ground where Quegg's carriage had been. In its place was a horse, dark as the night itself with glowing eyes, spurred on by a black, faceless rider. The horse reared up and then the rider spurred it on down the road – in pursuit of Quegg.

Simon Quegg was never seen again after that dreadful, stormy night. And it was a similar night that faced The Ghostbusters as they returned from one of their missions. Ray Stantz was at the wheel of ECTO-1, with his green ghosty-friend, Slimer, up there on his shoulder.

Peter, Egon and Winston knew that Ray was just a big kid at heart. They knew he always felt sorry for Slimer whenever he was scolded by Peter, or left out of things in general. So, it came as no surprise when they stopped at a coffee shop, and Ray ordered two dozen hamburgers to take-out just for the little green ghoulie, left behind in the Ectomobile.

The owner of the coffee shop may have raised an eyebrow or two — but, anyway, he reckoned, he needed the business. Stormy nights were usually bad for trade . . .

"We'll be out in a little while, Slimer!" Ray grinned, watching as the whole tray of hamburgers was shovelled into the ghosty-green mouth. It was good to see Slimer munching so happily.

Then, he stopped. Surely, Ray thought, that couldn't possibly be the sound of hooves pounding towards him, wheels rattling along the road?

"Whoa!" came a voice, and a horse-drawn buggy suddenly loomed out of the darkness. Ray could see an unhappy, haunted-looking man pulling at the reins trying to keep the restless horse under control.

"Can you tell me, sir," — even the voice sounded haunted — "how many miles it is to my home at Providence?"

Ray was surprised. "Providence, Rhode Island? It's 80 miles east from here!"

"What? But, Providence was only 20 miles west, when I left the inn!"

"I'm telling you the truth!" Ray insisted. "You've got to turn around and go 80 miles back east!"

"No!" The man glanced back in terror. "I cannot tarry any longer! It gains on me every minute! Yet, I must reach home tonight!"

A crack of the reins, and both horse and buggy were gone.

Then — more hoof beats, echoing strangely through the night, hot blasts of steaming breath . . . and a black-clad rider on horseback

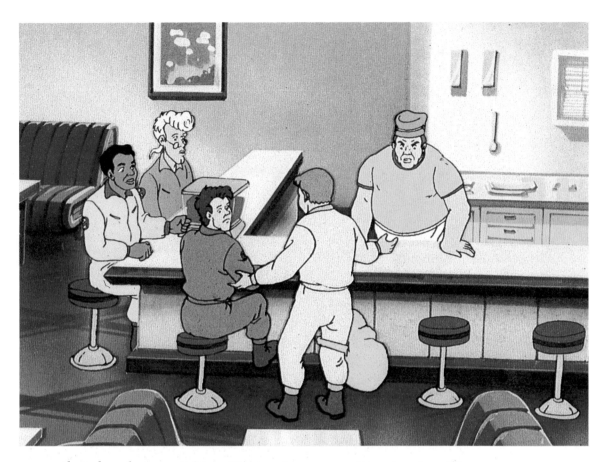

thundered past, making Slimer cling on to Ray for dear life.

"Slimer!" Ray yelled desperately, striding towards the coffee shop at the same time. "Slimer, let go!"

Dripping with rain, and with Slimer attached to his leg, Ray flung open the door. Peter, Egon and Winston were just finishing their coffee and hamburgers.

"Did you see them?" Ray demanded, a wild look in his eyes. "A man in old fashioned clothes, said he was trying to get to-to . . ."

"Providence?" finished the coffee shop owner. "That's just old Simon Quegg, our local ghost. Shows up on stormy nights, asking the way home, but never believes anyone when they tell him!"

"What about the other rider?" Ray persisted. "The one that followed Quegg?"

"You saw that?" Suddenly, the owner was a very frightened man.

"Well — yes."

"Only a handful of people have ever seen the Rider!" the man gabbled, bundling them all towards the door. "And disaster always follows! You've got to go!"

The door slammed, leaving The Ghostbusters staring blankly through the pouring rain, first at the "CLOSED" sign, then at each other.

"Come on!" yelled Winston, first to start running towards ECTO-1. "Let's get out of the rain!"

"Guys," said Ray, once they were all safely inside, "we've just got to find this Simon Quegg. Tonight. I saw the terrified look in his eyes . . . And all he wants is to go home!"

"From a scientific viewpoint," said Egon, already peering behind his specs for some sign of life on his PKE meter, "it might be interesting . . ."

On and on, Ray Stantz drove the Ectomobile through the raging storm. Egon was about to suggest calling the whole thing off and going home, when the needle suddenly jumped to a maximum Psycho Kinetic Energy reading.

"Stop!" he yelled, waking up Peter and Slimer. "Stop here!"

The Ghostbusters barely had time to put on their Proton Packs before the sound of galloping hooves, creaking wheels and the jingling of a horse's harness mingled with the sound of the pouring rain. Egon Spengler was always right.

"Gentlemen, please let me pass!" cried Quegg, reining his horse to a stop. "I must reach home before the night is out!"

"You asked me directions a little while ago," said Ray. "Remember?"

"Yes . . ." Quegg nodded in confusion. "You-you told me that Providence was . . . that it was . . ." He gave a dreadful moan, covering his face with a trembling hand. "Oh, why can't I find my way home?"

"Maybe we can help you," Ray suggested, more gently. "Just get down from the buggy!"

"I don't think he can, Ray," Egon interrupted. "It and the horse happen to be more powerful than he is! The Psycho Kinetic

Energy readings on the PKE meter are completely different!"

"Then," said Ray, adjusting his Proton Gun, "I'll have to trap the horse and buggy, without getting Quegg!"

"No!" screamed Quegg, already shaking the reins to get the horse moving. "I-I can hear it drawing closer, closer every minute . . ."

But Ray raised his gun and fired — right on target. Both the horse and the buggy began to glow brightly.

"Oh, no!" Egon looked up anxiously from his faithful PKE meter. "Ray, please stop! There's a danger of . . ."

His warning came only seconds too late. The proton beam bounced back and caught Ray, at the same moment as Quegg fell to the ground with a thump. And when the horse and buggy appeared again, they were carrying Ray Stantz away, into the darkness!

Then came the second, far more sinister sound of galloping hooves. A black horse and rider loomed out of nowhere, then soaring right above their heads, chased Ray on Quegg's ghost buggy.

Worse still, the night was lightening, soon it would be daybreak. Egon, Peter and Winston all knew there was no hope of finding Ray until dead of night, and only then if the weather was stormy again.

"I-I seem to remember . . ." They had almost forgotten! Quegg was still with them. "I have to return home . . ."

"Hey! You're not going anywhere!" cried Peter, poking a finger at him. "Ray risked his life to help you!"

"I did not ask for his help!" Quegg retorted. "Now, I must go in this direction . . . Or, is it that way? I don't . . . I don't know . . ."

"I think, Mr. Quegg," said Egon, "we have to help each other. You help us find Ray, and we'll help you get home!"

Not that Quegg *was* much help, as they soon discovered, back at the Ghostbusters' HQ.

"I've told you everything I know!" he kept saying irritably. Slimer lashed out at him every five minutes. There was no doubt he blamed Quegg for losing his friend.

The weather forecast didn't sound too hopeful, either.

"Just a cloudy night!" Winston announced, following the umpteenth call to the weather station. "No rain or thunderstorms!"

"Have to make our own, then!" said Egon, coming in with a small tank, complete with a hose, nozzle and a control box on the side. "Just as soon as it's dark!"

"Yeah," said Winston, "but there's no guarantee Ray and the buggy will appear, just because we've created our own rain!"

"Mr. Quegg is our guarantee," said Egon, his eyes firmly on the disgruntled ghost. "He's the one who belongs on that buggy, after all!"

At long last, it was time to return to the spot where Ray had disappeared. Everyone clambered into ECTO-1. Slimer was looking very pleased with himself — he had been given a special job to do.

"How can you make it rain?" Quegg couldn't help asking.

"See Egon's special device?" said Winston. "That's filled with silver iodide! Spray it on the right kind of clouds, and, if you're lucky — boom! It rains!"

There was a loud rumble, and out of the back of ECTO-1 roared ECTO-2, The Ghostbusters' helicopter, piloted by Egon Spengler. And, who should be the co-pilot? Why, none other than Slimer, complete with helmet and goggles, and squealing delightedly as the helicopter soared into the sky.

"You know what to do, Slimer?" asked Egon, after a few minutes.

Slimer nodded enthusiastically, turning the dial back and forth on Egon's tank-machine, and setting it on HIGH.

"Okay Slimer! Push the button!"

Swelling with importance, Slimer pointed the nozzle down over the side of the helicopter and pushed the button on the control box.

A strong blast of yellow powder shot out with such force that he was torn from his safety strap and launched into the air, Egon and ECTO-2 both tumbling towards the ground.

It was only by sheer guts and some good luck that Egon kept control of the helicopter – but Slimer was not so fortunate. All he

could do was to hang on to Egon's rain-maker, a trail of yellow powder lacing through the clouds behind him, until the last puff of silver iodide was gone, and he fell out of the sky.

This time, his luck was in. He landed on something soft. Dr Peter Venkman to be precise, covering him with green slime – just as he'd done on Peter's first-ever ghostbusting job.

"Slimer!" he growled. He had never quite forgiven the little green ghoul.

A huge fork of lightning followed by a loud crash of thunder made them all look up, rain was beginning to pour down by the bucket-load. Peter Venkman was soaked through in a matter of minutes!

"Someone talk me into finding another job!" he growled, with one last glare in Slimer's direction.

But the sound of galloping hooves and the creak of buggy wheels soon made him and the other two Ghostbusters hold their breath, hoping against hope that Ray Stantz would be on board the ghost ride.

And, so he was! Wide-eyed, worn out – but still in one piece!

"Boy!" he sighed. "Am I glad to see you guys?" He tried to dismount the buggy, but – as with Quegg – some strange force seemed to hold him back.

"No! Don't zap the buggy!" Ray cried out in alarm, seeing Winston's Proton Gun at the ready. "I tried that, and look where it got me!"

"Because you fired alone!" Egon shouted back. "If we fire our three proton beams all together, we should stand a better chance!"

So much for looking on the bright side . . . Three Proton Guns fired towards the horse and buggy – but nothing happened!

"The lightning must have overloaded our Proton Packs!" yelled Egon. "It's caused short circuits all round!"

"We must leave!" shrieked Quegg. Already they could hear the devilish horse and the black rider approaching. "We must not stay here!"

"Maybe that's just what we should do!" Ray roared back at him, the black rider thundering nearer. "For so long, that rider has chased you, kept you from going home! So, break the cycle! Get back on the buggy with me, and we'll face him together!"

Nobody said anything. But, at that moment, everyone there realised what a brave little guy Ray Stantz actually was, including Quegg.

"Perhaps you are right, Mr Stantz," he nodded at last, climbing up and taking the reins from Ray's hands.

Meanwhile the black rider was galloping closer and closer . . .

A sudden flash of lightning made the mysterious rider lift his head – and Simon Quegg could not have been more astounded.

"Th-that's my face!" he gasped, seeing the hideous lips, the evil smile. "I-I've been running away from – from myself!"

"Forgive me, Mr Stantz," he went on, pushing Ray down from the buggy. "But, I must do this alone!"

"Faster! Faster!" he yelled, cracking the reins like fury – until the two riders and two horses met, passing right through each other.

There was a strong gust of wind, and a whirlpool of ectoplasmic material swirled up into the sky like a tornado, blowing the clouds and the rain away to reveal a clear bright moon.

And, through the beautiful, peaceful night, came the sound of a horse and buggy trotting along, Simon Quegg holding the reins.

"I had to come back and thank you, Mr Stantz," he smiled happily. "You gave me the courage to see that the rider was me — the cruel, selfish man I have always been. And now — now, Mr Stantz I can at last go home!"

THE HOLE
IN THE WALL
GANG

"All right, Egon!" cried Ray Stantz, as The Ghostbusters speeded along in their Ectomobile. "What's the job, this time?"

"Cheese!"

"Cheese?"

"Limburger cheese! Charles Von Limburger is the heir to the world's largest cheese fortune! He's also been landed with a haunted mansion . . ."

"A haunted mansion?" Somehow, thought Peter Venkman, it all sounded just a bit corny. "Well – at least, we know . . ."

But, even he had to admit that the place looked the part, with spires and towers and domes casting black shadows all around the stormy landscape. Even the front door opened with a series of tooth-griding creaks and groans.

"Yes?"

Ray had to look twice before he saw the tiny man standing in front of him.

"Oh – er, hi! We're The Ghostbusters!"

"Oh, yes!" The man certainly seemed pleased to see them and showed them inside. "Come right in! I'm Charles Von Limburger! And this," he went on, extending a hand towards a woman who seemed to tower above him, "is Lady Limburger!"

Egon wondered if they ought to shake hands, but Von Limburger was already leading the way into a huge room. Dark and mysterious shadows hovered all around.

"We moved here three weeks ago," Limburger was saying, "and we've been experiencing strange supernatural manifestations ever since!"

"Crashing and banging," added his wife, "howlings and moanings, and the most frightful gruntings and things falling out of cupboards . . ."

The Ghostbusters glanced at each other. It seemed like they'd heard it all before.

"We-we've seen them lurking in the dark," Limburger continued

in a frightened whisper. "Huge, red-eyed monsters, with scrabbling claws . . ."

"Moaning and scratching at the walls," Lady Limburger chimed in.

"Rustling in the shadows, and wailing in the dungeons . . ."

"Psycho Kinetic Energy readings indicate that the source of the trouble is upstairs!" interrupted Egon, consulting his PKE meter.

"Well," said Limburger, "goodbye, then!"

"We've decided to leave the house for the week-end," Lady Limburger explained. "So as to give you a chance to do your job without us being in the way!"

They had grabbed their luggage and disappeared, even before a fast-talking Ghostbuster like Peter Venkman could think of anything to say.

"Right!" said Egon, breaking the stunned silence. "Let's get to work!"

"I was afraid you'd say that!" groaned Winston — but he began

following Egon up the wide Limburger staircase all the same, humping Proton Packs, PKE meters and ghost traps, along with Peter and Ray.

"Okay," he whispered, as a door at the end of the corridor loomed towards them. "This is the last chance for anyone to have a bad feeling!"

Egon pushed the door open, and The Ghostbusters found themselves looking into a huge bedroom, the furniture covered in white sheets.

"It's in here!" Egon nodded slowly, pointing a finger towards a wall. "This is it . . .!"

"A hole in the wall?" gasped Ray in stunned disbelief. "You must be kidding, Egon! Hello?" he shouted putting his face in the hole. "Come out, come out, wherever you are . . ."

And nobody was more surprised than Ray when something *did* come out! Sixty pounds of slime, to be precise, hitting his face at forty miles an hour!

"Oh, boy!" Peter grinned. "I must be the lucky one, today! I'm usually the one who gets slimed."

Poor old Peter! He spoke too soon. The next moment a great mass of slime came shooting out of the hole and hit him on the back of the neck!

"Well," he said, turning around, "at least it didn't hit me in the face!"

Splat! Being slimed twice on one job was enough to make any self-respecting Ghostbuster reach for his Proton Pack.

"Okay!" Peter yelled, firing his Proton Gun. "Eat purple death, cold slime!"

"Peter," said Egon warningly, "that may not be such a good idea . . ."

But a bright proton beam had already streaked into the hole, crackling and fizzing and sparkling like it was Guy Fawkes Night.

Everything went quiet.

"Is that it?" asked Ray, somewhat disbelievingly. No job had ever been so easy! Maybe, Egon thought, Peter had done right, after all . . .

Only Winston saw a tiny ghost crawling out of the hole and land on the floor, only seconds before a rumble sounded from the other side . . .

"Aaaaagh – !"

"Yeeek – !"

"No-o-o-o-ooo!"

What else could The Ghostbusters say, with plaster falling, walls cracking, paintings sliding down from walls, and furniture toppling over?

Whilst all the time, the rumbling grew louder and louder, making the whole house shake, causing smaller holes to appear all over the place!

"Listen!" Ray yelled at last, pointing a finger. "It's coming right at us! Look!"

They all looked. It was just about the fiercest, ugliest, nastiest

ghost any of them had seen in a long, long time . . . all six inches of it!

And yet, that mini ghost seemed to be an absolute whizz at dodging the beams from Peter's Proton Gun. Again and again he fired. And, again and again, that nasty little spook escaped. And each time Peter fired and missed he smashed another hole in the wall. Until, at last — zap! Their ghost trap opened with a deadly glow, and all was quiet.

But, once the smoke from Winston's gun had cleared, that was when The Ghostbusters saw the full extent of the damage . . . Holes in the walls, the floor, the ceiling . . .

And, as if that weren't enough, tiny little ghosts began coming out of every single one, until The Ghostbusters could hardly move. Mini ghosts were sitting on the equipment, riding on their shoes and Proton Packs — they were everywhere they looked!

"There's something horrible in that hole!" pronounced Egon. Even one little ghost was shuddering in fear. "I must send in a probe!"

Lucky The Ghostbusters had a no-nonsense guy like Winston in the team. He soon set about widening the hole with his bare hands, whilst Peter brought in a mini-helicopter, ready for Ray to fix on a remote control unit and TV camera.

"Okay, Peter," said Ray at last, unwinding a huge coil of cable. "Whenever you're ready!"

"Careful with those cables, Ray," Peter warned, working the controls to send the mini helicopter up in the air, then into the hole.

"No problem!" Ray grinned cheerfully. But, he spoke too soon . . .

In one single instant, the cables were taut, then began spinning off the reel so fast that Ray only just managed to grab the end!

"Yee-oo-www-rrrgggh – !" he yelled – which is about all anyone can say when they are being yanked headlong into a hole in a wall, then out again, scattering splinters of wood, slabs of plaster, little green ghoulies – and three Ghostbusters – all over the place.

"What did you see, Ray?" demanded Winston, once they'd all got their breath back. "And what happened to your hair?"

"I saw the supernatural world . . ." Ray's voice sounded supernatural, too. "The Outer Limits . . . The Twilight Zone . . ."

"Come on guys," Egon interrupted. "We'd best inspect the damage!"

Walls blown out . . . Wreckage everywhere . . . There was hardly anything left worth inspecting. Not unless you counted holes. Millions and trillions of holes, all with little green ghosties piling out.

The only thing Winston could find intact was one small piece of wood panelling. And even that had a knot hole in it, with a green mini ghost squirting through.

And when he tried shaking the green ghost off, still more tiny ghosts came oozing out, intent on following the first one!

"Hey!" Winston was clearly enthralled. "Hey, fellas, look!"

"Of course!" cried Egon. "The size of the hole determines the size of the ghosts! The smaller the hole, the smaller the ghosts!"

"So, the bigger the hole," Ray added thoughtfully, "the bigger the ghost gets . . ."

"Wow . . ." breathed Winston. "That hole over there, it's so big, there's not much wall left for it to be a hole in!"

Egon was already turning pale. "I don't even want to think about the size of the ghost that could come through that hole!"

"I don't think you'll have time to think!" Ray yelled above the menacing tread of thundering footsteps, getting nearer every minute. "Here it comes!"

"Proton Guns at the ready!" commanded Egon. "Fire!"

Ion beams streaked out without stopping. It was only when the smoke had cleared that all four Ghostbusters realised the dreadful truth.

All they had done was to make one enormous hole even more enormous, spreading up to the ceiling, down towards the floor, and out into the next-door rooms, almost as far as the eye could see!

And – judging by the footsteps which were pounding loud enough to set the whole Limburger mansion shaking like a bowl of jelly in an earthquake – there was still worse to come!

"Egon," gulped Peter Venkman bravely. "I-I think it's time to put Plan B into operation!"

"Plan B . . .?" echoed Ray and Winston.

"Run!" bellowed Peter, already going like a champion sprinter.

The Limburger mansion was still shaking and shuddering, quaking and quivering, when the team skidded to a breathless halt outside.

Then, suddenly, yet slowly, with a whole lot of creaking and crashing and banging, the entire mansion collapsed like a giant pack of cards.

All The Ghostbusters could see was a huge pile of rubble. Every one of the little green ghosts had disappeared. Or, so they thought . . .

"The hole is still there, under all that rubble," Egon told them,

his PKE meter pointing straight down, above the smoking ruin which remained. "Only now, it's fifty feet across . . ."

"F-fifty feet?" stammered Ray Stantz.

"That means," Peter joined in, "that whatever comes out of that hole will be the biggest thing we've ever seen . . ."

His words faltered to a stop, as the ground began rumbling beneath their feet, and a gigantic, clawed hand scrabbled free!

The Ghostbusters soon saw that this was on the end of a huge, gigantic arm which reached all round as if it couldn't wait to make a grab at something.

"Can't we give it a peace offering?" suggested Peter, trying to be funny, as usual. He hardly expected Winston to start delving into his pockets!

"Hey!" he shouted. "I've still got that piece of wood panelling with the knot-hole in it!"

"Throw it away, Winston!" Ray snapped impatiently, whirling

around as Egon gave an excited yell.

"Ray, you're brilliant! Throw that hole into the big hole, Winston! It's our only hope!"

By now, another hand was emerging, dust and rubble flying all around. But Winston didn't flinch once, not even when the gigantic head finally burst through, baring a whole mouthful of deadly-looking fangs.

"Well, well!" he heard himself saying. "Quite a big one, aren't you?"

The monster ghost roared in reply — and this was Winston's Big Chance!

He flung the piece of wood with the hole in it right down the enormous gullet, then fled for cover.

It was enough to make any monster's face curdle. The beast shrunk, shrivelled and withered all at once, fast sinking back into the hole in the ground with a last few pathetic-sounding cries.

Still the ground shook and shivered, quaked and quivered. Then came the loudest explosion any of them had ever heard, resounding for hundreds of miles around.

But, when the Limburgers drew up in the limousine, it was clear they were none too impressed.

"Where is our house?" demanded Lady Limburger.

"It was a bigger job than we expected!" explained Peter. "We'll send you our bill in the morning!"

Ray Stantz could hear Lady Limburger raging as he took the wheel of ECTO-1.

"That's what you get for hiring a bunch of amateurs! Next time, call the REAL Ghostbusters!"

XMAS MARKS
THE SPOT

Peter Venkman didn't believe in Christmas. All that snow people sang about, the cosy fires and the present-giving around the tree . . . It just wasn't his favourite time of year.

"His Dad was always away on business at Christmas," Ray told Egon and Winston. "That affects a kid after a while!"

"Easier to shrug off by pretending you don't care," agreed Egon.

"Pretend long enough," added Winston, "and soon you believe it!"

Well, anyway, it was Peter who took things like jobs on Christmas Eve in his stride. Even if that meant trying to find a telephone when the Ectomobile broke down at the foot of a snow-covered hill. A hill which — suddenly — seemed a whole lot steeper than it looked.

Suddenly, the whole landscape began shimmering, like a strange mirage on the desert sand, flashing on and off, on and off.

It was sharp-eyed Winston who noticed the gas-lamps first, glowing yellow through a break in the snow, shining down on

cobbled streets, on frost gilding the arched doorways, on sloping roofs and attic windows . . .

"Wow . . ." breathed Ray, hardly able to believe his eyes. "This place is ancient, like something out of Victorian England!"

"Too old for a telephone?" argued Peter. "You wait and see!"

Heads bent against the bitterly cold wind, The Ghostbusters barely heard the hansom cabs rumbling along, paid little attention to the gentlemen in frocked coats and top hats nodding to one another as they passed a group of lantern-lit carol-singers . . .

How about that butcher's shop in the distance, Peter wondered, the one where a kind-faced man and his crippled son were carrying a small goose out into the frosty night? Would there be a telephone there that they could use?

But, it was tough going. They had only gone a little way along the dimly-lit street, when an echo of the most nerve-shattering, hideous moaning seemed to make their hair stand on end.

"What the heck was that?" asked Winston.

"Sounds like it came from a house over there!" Ray shouted, pointing down a dark, narrow lane.

"Picking up strong Psycho Kinetic Energy readings from inside!" nodded Egon, looking up from his PKE meter. "Right up there!"

The words had barely left his mouth, when the ghost of a man flew out from an upstairs window, trailing chains, iron boxes and lead weights behind him as he rose into the air.

"I'm getting plenty more readings!" Egon yelled, pointing upwards. "Big and powerful! Right there!"

Sure enough, three more spooks were already zooming in towards an open window, a series of flashes coming from inside the room!

"No!" screamed a tormented voice. "Go away! What do you want of me?"

"Oh, boy," sighed Peter, reaching for his Proton Pack. "Seems a Ghostbuster's work is never done!"

All four stormed in through the front door, rushing past the big, heavy doorknocker. They paid no attention to the desperate cries of the ghost they had seen seconds before. "No! I, Jacob Marley, I tell you — leave the house of Ebeneezer Scrooge! No-o-o-o-o — !" it shrieked after them.

But The Ghostbusters were already racing through the dusty, dark, old house, Proton Guns at the ready, straight across the hall, and into the bedroom.

Then, they stopped, reeling back in surprise. There, in front of them, were three ghosts. One, a young girl, dressed in a bright tunic and surrounded by the brightest light any of them had ever seen. The second wearing a long, brown robe trimmed with fur. The third draped and mysteriously hooded. And Scrooge.

"Well, don't just stand there!" he cackled. "Do something!"

There came a cry of despair and anguish from the ghosts. "Young Sirs, no!"

"Release us! Or you and all Christmasses to come will pay the price!"

But ion beams were already streaking out into the gloom, with Egon pulling out the ghost trap from under his jacket, ready to slide across the floor.

The doors to the trap opened, then closed, the three Ghosts of Christmas safely inside. The job, it seemed, couldn't have been easier.

"You've beaten them!" cried Scrooge in delight. "Gentlemen, what you've done here tonight . . ."

"Is worth every penny!" finished Peter, writing out a bill. "If you'd like to make your cheque payable to The Ghostbusters . . ."

"Money?" screeched Scrooge in disbelief. "You charge money for this?" He scrabbled inside a battered purse and flung a gold coin at their feet. "This I'll pay, and not a shilling more!"

"Hey! A half sovereign, in mint condition!" Ray's eyes gleamed.

"Thanks a lot, Mr Scrooge!"

The Ghostbusters found the hill a whole lot easier going down than when they'd come up, but the night was still very cold, with the promise of more snow to come.

They were all glad to pile into ECTO-1. Ray flicked the ignition switch, but without much hope. Nobody was more surprised than he was when the engine purred into life without any trouble. Everyone clapped and cheered at the thought of going home.

Everyone, that is, except Egon.

"I keep thinking there's something very familiar about what happened," he kept saying, all the way back to Ghostbusters' HQ. "As if it's all happened somewhere before . . ."

"Okay if you go and unload the ghost trap in the containment unit, Egon?" asked Ray when they arrived home. "We're taking Peter to get a Christmas tree!"

"A tree?" echoed Janine, their secretary. "For Christmas? Huh!"

"But – I thought you liked Christmas, Janine," said Egon, puzzled.

There didn't seem to be much Christmas spirit in the streets of New York, either. Every time Winston called out: "Hi! Merry Christmas!" – back came the same answer. "Bah! Humbug!" – usually to a chorus of loud grumbles and cars tooting their horns impatiently.

And instead of garlands and fairy lights, the face of Ebeneezer Scrooge appeared everywhere – on hundreds of books in the shop windows, all entitled "A CHRISTMAS HUMBUG, BY EBENEEZER SCROOGE".

"Scrooge?" cried Peter. "But – he s the guy we helped! So, how could we help him, unless – unless we went back in time . . ."

"Those ghosts we trapped," said Winston, "they must have been the ghosts of Christmas Past, Christmas Present, and Christmas Future!"

"Everyone knows that story!" snarled a passer-by. "In 1837,

55

Scrooge defeated the three Christmas ghosts, and put an end to Christmas. And good riddance!"

"We went back in time," Ray Stantz gasped in horror. "And, by changing the past — we've changed the present!"

"No problem," said Peter. "We took the ghosts, all we have to do is put them back."

"But Egon's about to unload them into the containment unit!" yelled Winston, beginning to panic. "We-we've got to stop him!"

Too late! Egon had just pulled the final switch as they raced down to the basement, drawing out the empty ghost trap with grim satisfaction.

"Scrooge's three ghosts are safely inside!" he nodded. "Okay?"

"No!" wailed Peter. "Oh, Egon, we just killed Christmas! It's gone forever, unless we can go back in time and return them to Scrooge's place!"

Egon gave a tiny moan. He just knew he'd been through the whole scene before.

"I'll have to make a hairline crack in the containment grid," he said at last. "Then I'll go inside the unit, and if I get the ghosts, I'll see you at Scrooge's. I've got about an hour, at the very most."

"And, if you don't make it?" Winston felt he just had to know.

"Then you will have to become the three ghosts of Christmas!"

It was an action replay . . . The snow-covered streets, ECTO-1 shuddering to a halt, the three Ghostbusters climbing to the top of a hill, the glow of the gas lamps, the crooked windows, arched doorways . . .

Only this time, Scrooge was looking quite pleased with himself, sitting at a desk with a quill pen.

"A Christmas Humbug . . ." he muttered as he wrote. "By Ebeneezer Scrooge! My, I do like the ring of that!"

And, yet — it was so difficult to concentrate. First, he thought he heard strange noises in the still, cold night. Then, strange, white shapes flitting by his window.

"H-hello?" he cried out, half in fear. "Wh-who is there?"

He waited, the silence seeming to cut into his very soul, like a knife. Then came a blood-curdling cry, an eerie figure in a white tunic crashed into the room and landed on top of him.

"Yaaaaggh!" Peter wasn't really sure that this was how a Christmas ghost should sound, but he was determined to do his best.

"Wh-what are you?" blustered Scrooge, glasses slipping down from his crooked nose. "Who do you think you are?"

"I'm Peter — " Venkman coughed hurriedly. "I mean, I am the ghost of Christmas Past!"

"B-but, you were defeated! I saw it myself! If you are the ghost of Christmas Past, where is the glow which surrounds you?"

"Oh, yeah . . ." Peter muttered remembering the lightning device in his costume. "Let's see, where's that switch . . ."

And for once, Peter lit up with the spirit of Christmas, gleaming and sparkling all over the place, glinting into Scrooge's beady eyes.

"And now, Scrooge," he said, taking out some picture-view

binoculars from underneath his robe, "how about a trip down Memory Lane?"

Back at Ghostbuster's HQ, Egon was putting the finishing touches to his Master Plan.

"Okay, Janine," he said at last. "Hit the button!"

A beam of light flashed from a device on the table to the containment unit, making a thin, hairline crack appear. Egon nodded, satisfied, and reached for a switch on his uniform.

"Oh, Egon!" Janine wailed in alarm. "Please – please be careful!"

Another flash of light, and Egon, now as thin and as wispy-looking as any of the ghosts, was sucked in through the crack. Janine could hardly bear it. Even Slimer seemed like great company just then.

And, at the same time as Egon found himself whirling and tumbling around looking for ghosts, Peter was whirling old Scrooge around in

a wheelchair, picture-view binoculars strapped to his mean, bony old head.

"Spirit," groaned Scrooge. "Can we not stop this – this flying, now?"

"Not – yet . . ." puffed Peter, reaching out to click the binoculars on to the next view. "Just keep looking through the magic window!"

"My old school!" breathed Scrooge. "I spent many a Christmas there, while my father was away. But, I had my books! What more did I need?"

"A lot more, I'd say," murmured Peter softly. "I know, I sure did. But, just because you had a rotten past, that's no reason to blame Christmas . . ." He heard his voice fading into nothing, listening to the words he had just spoken.

"I think," he said, "that's a lesson we could all stand to learn."

"Maybe," nodded Scrooge. "But, I am still not convinced!"

"Then, you've got two more chances!" Peter leapt on to the

window sill and gave a tug on the rope, ready for Ray and Winston to haul him up into the air.

None of them could know that, at that same moment, Egon was swimming through the sea of white mist which enclosed every one of the ghosts which The Ghostbusters had ever captured, trying desperately to find the right ones!

"The hour's almost over!" Janine screamed over the walkie-talkie. "Come back, Egon! You'll be trapped!"

"No, wait! There they are, Janine!" She could see him waving frantically to the Christmas ghosts on the TV monitor. "Hurry!" he called out to them. "Follow me!"

The effect of his words was amazing. Whole processions of ghostly characters and creatures began scrambling towards the hairline crack which would give them their freedom.

"Get to the grid device, Janine!" Egon yelled over the radio. "If they start to come through, turn it off! Don't let them escape!"

But, time was passing — and passing fast. By now, Winston was being Christmas Present, swinging from the rope with a very green-looking Scrooge, and pointing to the darkened city below!

"See them?" he demanded. "The workhouses where you send the poor?"

"N-no, spirit!" Scrooge's teeth chattered more than he did!

"Well, hang around! We'll swing past them again in just a second!"

"Hurry up, Egon — " Peter muttered, checking his watch. "Where are the *real* Christmas ghosts?"

He had no means of knowing it — but, even as he spoke, those ghosts were right behind Egon in the containment unit!

"Keep going!" he yelled at them. "Don't look back!"

Even Slimer was exhausted. But, at last, they were free — only a split second before Egon's device exploded in a shower of sparks and flashes.

"Inside!" Egon commanded, grabbing a ghost trap. "Please! It's faster!'

In a matter of moments, ECTO-2 left HQ, with Egon at the controls — and the ghost trap safely by his side.

Things at Scrooge's were now getting desperate. So desperate, that Ray Stantz, alias Christmas Present, was having to amuse Scrooge with a game of charades. Charades, of all things!

Then, a cry from the street below made Winston dash to the window.

"Look, Peter!" he cried. "It's Egon!"

And, so it was, racing along and waving madly with one hand, and holding up the ghost trap with the other.

"I got them!" he was yelling. "I got them!"

"Nice work, Egon!" Winston shouted back, unwinding the rope at the same time. "Now, catch!"

And, if Egon crashed through the window and sent everyone flying — well, so what? All that mattered was that the three ghosts of Christmas were back where they belonged, crawling thankfully out of the ghost trap.

"Why!" Scrooge squinted painfully, seeing the mass of cables entangling Egon. "Jacob Marley, still wearing the chains! Why have you returned?"

"To say that you will be visited this night by three spirits!"

"Three more?" Scrooge groaned. "I-I'm not sure I can stand it!"

"So much for all our hard work," said Ray. "I wonder if old Scrooge has learned his lesson?"

"Yes," came Christmas Present's voice. "I think he has."

"Just as I believe," he added, turning towards Peter, "you have learned yours."

"Yes," answered Peter, looking more serious than any of The Ghostbusters had ever seen him before. "Believe me, I have. I don't think I ever appreciated Christmas until I lost it. Now — can we go home?"

"You only had to ask!" Christmas Present gave a merry-sounding laugh, "Just take hold of my robe!"

None of The Ghostbusters ever really knew what happened next. They only remembered a sudden, blinding flurry of sparkling white snow. When it cleared, they were back inside the old fire station,

Janine and Slimer setting a bowl of punch on the table!

"How – how did we – ?" stammered Ray. "We were over at Scrooge's – "

"The question is," said Winston, "did it work? Is Christmas back?"

His answer came in a chorus of Good King Wenceslas from the street – then, the sound of sleigh bells tinkling through the frosty, night air.

"Come along, Dancer and Prancer. Donner and Blitzen!" came a voice.

"No . . ." said Peter, after a pause. "It couldn't be – could it?"

Then he laughed. A happy, child's laugh of the boyhood he had never known.

"Then, again – why not? Merry Christmas, everyone!"